You Think It's Fun to Be a Clown!

CIRCUS TONIGHT
5:00 to 7:30 p.m.

YOU THINK IT'S FUN TO BE A CLOWN!

by DAVID A. ADLER

Pictures by RAY CRUZ

Doubleday & Company, Inc. Garden City, New York

With love
to my Renée
and our Michael
—DAVID ADLER

To B. K.
—RAY CRUZ

Library of Congress Cataloging in Publication Data

Adler, David A
You think it's fun to be a clown!

SUMMARY: Describes in rhymed text some of the disadvantages of being a clown.
[1. Clowns—Fiction. 2. Stories in rhyme]
I. Cruz, Ray. II. Title.
PZ8.3.A2327Yo [E] 79-7594

ISBN: 0-385-14459-8 Trade
0-385-14460-1 Prebound

Printed in the United States of America
9 8 7 6 5 4 3 2

Inside…

Outside,

Coming down.

You think it's fun
to be a clown?

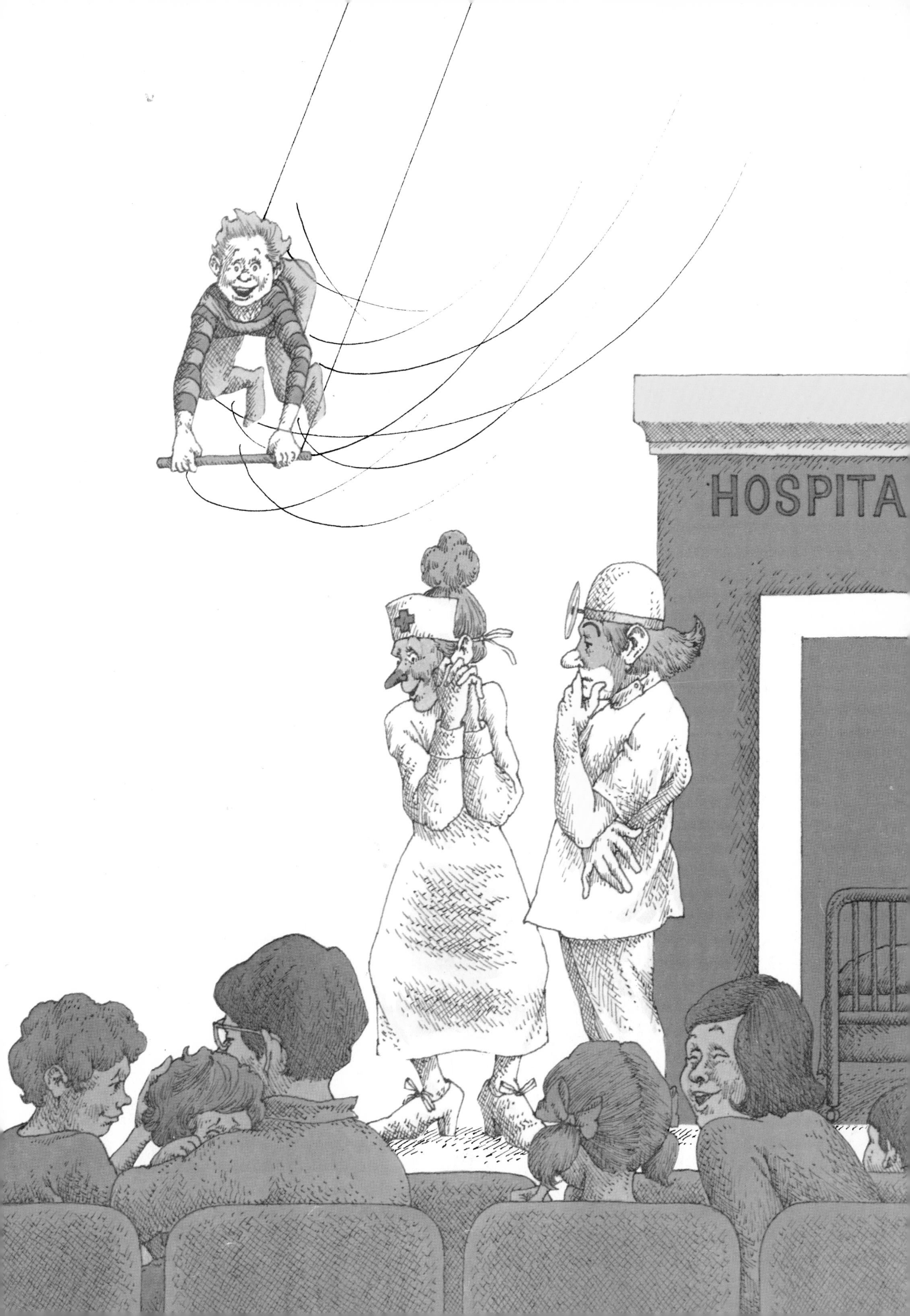
HOSPITA

I'm
scared
to jump.

I hate
to fall.

Clowning is
no fun at all!

Stepped on,

Shot at,

Cut in half,

Just to make

some people laugh.

First I'm riding,

Then I'm walking,

But I'm never
ever talking.

Look how many

clowns we are,

Squeezed inside
of just one car.

Lions chase me,

Tigers scare me,

Elephants
wash me clean.

I feel so clean.

EEEK! I'm dirty!

I'm so glad it's

seven-thirty.

Now I can be . . .

me!